The Brothers Grimm

Hansel and Gretel

and other fairy tales

Miles Kelly

First published in 2015 by Miles Kelly Publishing Ltd
Harding's Barn, Bardfield End Green, Thaxted, Essex, CM6 3PX, UK

2 4 6 8 10 9 7 5 3

Publishing Director Belinda Gallagher
Creative Director Jo Cowan
Editorial Director Rosie Neave
Designer Rob Hale
Production Elizabeth Collins, Caroline Kelly
Reprographics Stephan Davis, Jennifer Cozens, Thom Allaway
Assets Lorraine King

ISBN 978-1-78209-747-1

Printed in China

British Library Cataloguing-in-Publication Data
A catalogue record for this book is available from the British Library

ACKNOWLEDGEMENTS
The publishers would like to thank the following artists who have contributed to this book:

Front cover and all border illustrations: Louise Ellis (The Bright Agency)

Inside illustrations:
Hansel and Gretel Atyeh Zeighami (Advocate-art)
The Poor Miller's Boy and the Cat Ayesha Lopez (Advocate-art)
The Wolf and the Seven Little Kids Kristina Swarner (The Bright Agency)
Foundling Claudia Venturini (Plum Pudding Illustration Agency)

Made with paper from a sustainable forest

www.mileskelly.net
info@mileskelly.net

Contents

Hansel
and
Gretel

Long ago, a woodcutter lived in a forest with his two children, a little boy called Hansel and a little girl called Gretel. The children's mother had died, and the woodcutter had married again, but his second wife was an evil woman who did not like Hansel and Gretel.

The family were very poor – so poor that the time came when they didn't have enough to eat. "What is to become of us?" the woodcutter sighed to his wife one night. "We can't feed the children, let alone ourselves."

"I'll tell you what," said his wife, "early tomorrow morning, we will take the children deep into the forest and leave them there. They will never find their way home again and we will be rid of them."

The woodcutter was horrified by this plan, but his wife muttered wicked words into his ear all night until he reluctantly agreed.

The couple had no idea that the children

were awake and had heard everything! Their tummies were too empty for them to sleep. Gretel sobbed but Hansel said: "Don't worry, I know what to do." He put on his coat and quietly slipped out of the house. He collected as many white pebbles as he could fit into a little bag. Then he crept back inside and said to Gretel, "We will be all right, I promise." The children wrapped their arms around each other and sat like that for the rest of the night.

Just before sunrise, the woman got the children up. "We're going into

the forest to fetch
firewood," she ordered. She gave
Gretel a chunk of bread to share with Hansel
for lunch, and off they set. But every now
and again, when the wicked woman wasn't
looking, Hansel dropped a white pebble from

his bag, to show him the way back.

When they had reached the middle of the forest, the woman lit a fire. "Stay here while your father and I go to fetch more wood," she said, and away they walked through the trees.

Of course, they didn't come back. The children waited until night fell, but there was no sign of them. Gretel was afraid and began to cry, but Hansel took her by the hand and followed the white pebbles which gleamed in the moonlight – all the way back home.

Their stepmother was shocked to see them, although she pretended she was delighted and made a fuss of them, saying: "Oh my darlings, I lost you in the forest, I have been heartbroken!" But that night she

8

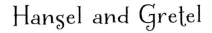

again told her husband that the children had to go – the very next day, they were to be abandoned even deeper in the forest.

Once again, Hansel and Gretel were awake and heard everything. Hansel got up and went to pick up pebbles as he had done before – but the woman had locked the door!

"Don't cry, Gretel," he told his sister, hugging her. "We'll think of something."

Early next morning, the woman once again gave Gretel a chunk of bread to share for lunch with her brother and led them off into the forest. As they walked, every now and again Gretel crumbled a little of the bread on the path, to show the way back.

Again the woman left the children by a

fire and again they waited till nightfall. Then they searched for the trail of bread – but they could find no trace of it! The birds had eaten every last crumb!

"Never mind," Hansel comforted Gretel, "maybe we can find the way on our own."

They walked the whole night and all through the next day – but they could not find their way out of the forest. Then suddenly they glimpsed a little house through the trees. They couldn't believe their eyes! It was built of cake, with a bread roof and windows of clear sugar! The starving children ran to it at once, broke bits off and tucked in. How delicious it tasted!

Suddenly the door opened and an old

woman came hobbling out on a stick. She bent down to peer closely at the two shivering children, for she could not see well at all. Hansel and Gretel were terribly frightened, but the old woman said kindly: "Oh, you dear children, are you lost? Do come in. I will look after you." She gave them milk and pancakes, then showed them to two little beds to rest.

Hansel and Gretel were so tired that they happily went straight to sleep. They didn't know that the old woman was actually a witch who ate children! As soon as the brother and sister had fallen asleep, she seized Hansel and locked him in a cage. He screamed and screamed and Gretel woke up and came running. Then the witch forced Gretel to fetch water and cook a meal for Hansel, for she wanted to fatten him up, ready for eating.

Every day, the witch forced Gretel to do hard tasks around the house. She had to cook fine food for Hansel, while she lived off nothing but crab shells. Every morning the witch hobbled to the cage and cried: "Hansel, stick out your finger so I can feel if you will soon be fat." And every morning Hansel stuck out a little chicken bone, so she thought he was still thin.

Four weeks passed and the witch grew tired of waiting. "Right, time for a tasty meal of little boy," she announced one day, licking her lips. "First, we'll bake some bread. Girl – go and climb inside the oven, to see if it is hot enough." The wicked old woman meant to shut Gretel in and cook her first!

But Gretel was clever and said: "Climb inside the oven? I'm not sure what you mean. Can't you do it first, to show me?"

The old witch groused and grumbled and shuffled up and stuck her head in the oven. Then Gretel gave her a mighty push and – *clang!* – she shut and bolted the door. The witch was trapped inside!

The brave little girl raced to the cage and set Hansel free. How they danced for joy! They filled their pockets with the witch's treasure and raced off into the forest.

As they ran, the trees became familiar – and at last they saw their father's cottage. To their delight, he rushed out to meet them without his horrible wife, for she had fallen ill and died. Their father had been miserable without them – he didn't know how he had ever let his wife leave them in the forest, though he suspected she must have put him under some sort of evil spell. Hansel and Gretel emptied their pockets and showed their father that they would never have to worry about money again. And they all lived happily ever after.

The Poor Miller's Boy and the Cat

Once upon a time there lived a miller who had neither a wife nor a child. Three young men worked for him as apprentices, learning the miller's trade. One day, after they had been with the miller for several years, he said to them: "I am old and cannot work forever. I want each of you three to go out and find a horse. I will give the mill to whoever brings back the best one."

The very next day, all three lads set out down the road on their quest. They walked till it was nightfall without finding any horses. Then they found a cave to sleep in for the night. But the two older apprentices had hatched a nasty plan. They got up while the third, younger, apprentice was sleeping and went on their way, leaving him in the cave.

Eric (for that was the youngest apprentice's name) woke up very upset to find himself all alone. He wandered out of the cave and set off sadly down the road once more. As he walked, he met a small grey cat which said, quite kindly, "Eric, I know what you are looking for."

Eric was too astonished to speak, so the cat continued.

"You want to find a beautiful horse," the cat said. "Come with me and work as my servant for seven years, then I will give you one more beautiful than you have ever seen in your whole life."

'Well, this certainly is an amazing cat', thought Eric to himself. 'Maybe she is speaking the truth…'

So he went along with her to her enchanted castle, which was filled with cat servants. They leapt nimbly upstairs and

downstairs, and all seemed very happy.

In the evening, Eric and the grey cat sat down to dinner. Three of the cat servants played music while they ate: one blew the bassoon, the other bowed the fiddle, and the third puffed out his cheeks at the trumpet.

"Now take him to bed," the grey cat ordered. One cat carried a candle and led Eric to his bedroom. Another cat pulled his shoes off, a second cat took his stockings off, and another cat turned down the bedclothes and blew out the candle.

The next morning, the cats returned and helped Eric out of bed. One put his stockings on, another slipped his feet into his shoes, one washed his face and dried it with her tail. 'Oh, I could get used to this', Eric thought, happily.

But then it was his turn to start work. The grey cat said she wanted Eric to chop wood every day. She gave him a silver axe – and that's what he did. He stayed living with the cats and worked hard, and he was very content. Once, the grey cat asked him to harvest the wheat in her fields. And once, she asked him to build her a small house. And the seven years passed by as swiftly as if they were seven months.

Then the grey cat asked Eric if he would like to see her horses.

"Oh, yes please," said Eric.

The grey cat opened the door of her stables and there stood twelve horses, so bright and shining, that his heart leapt at the sight of them.

"Now return to the mill," said the grey cat, "and in three days I will bring you a horse."

Eric trusted the cat and he trudged off down the road back to the mill.

The other two apprentices had returned long ago, each dragging an old nag behind them. They sneered at Eric and mocked him when they saw him coming. After all, Eric was without a horse – and he was still dressed in the same dirty smock that he had been wearing when they last saw him seven years ago! The two apprentices even said he was too ragged to come into the mill to eat. Instead, they gave him a tiny morsel of supper to have in the barn, where he had to spend the night on the hay.

However, Eric didn't mind.

The next morning, three days had passed since he had left the grey cat. As the sun rose, a golden coach came driving up to the mill,

pulled by six gleaming horses. Behind, a
groom rode a seventh.

The coach came to a stop outside the
barn, and a beautiful princess got out of it. To
Eric's amazement the princess spoke to him.
She said: "I was the little grey cat whom you
served faithfully for seven years! Now, I will
reward you richly for all your hard work."

She clapped her hands for her butler to come forward. He unpacked royal clothes and dressed Eric in them. When Eric was ready, he looked more handsome than any prince! Then the princess strode off to find the miller. She asked to see the horses the other two apprentices had brought home with them. They were a very sorry sight – one was blind and the other was lame!

Then the princess ordered her groom to show the seventh horse – which she had brought for Eric.

The miller admired the wonderful horse. "The mill belongs to Eric," he said, reaching out for the reins.

But the princess shook her head. "Keep

your little mill," she said, "and the horse." Then she showed Eric into her golden carriage and drove away with him. They went straight to the little house which he had built and Eric saw that it had turned magically into a magnificent castle, filled with treasures. He was richer than he could ever have dreamt! There, he and the princess were married, and they lived happily ever after. So let no one ever say that the best stories have sad endings.

The Wolf and the Seven Little Kids

Once upon a time there lived a mother goat who had seven little kids. One day, she wanted to go into the forest to fetch some food. So she called the seven little kids to her and said: "Be on your guard against the wolf – if you let him in, he will gobble you up! If he comes here, he may disguise himself to try and trick you. But you will know it is him because he has a rough voice and black feet."

"Don't worry about us, Mother," bleated the little kids, "we will be fine."

So the mother goat took up her basket and set off into the forest.

After a while, someone came knocking at the door and called out, "Open the door, dear children. It is your mother – I have brought you something tasty to eat."

But the voice was rough…

"No, we will not open the door!" the little kids shouted in reply. "Our mother has a soft, kind, gentle voice. You must be the wolf!"

Then the wolf went away and ate a whole jar of honey, to make his voice soft. He came back, knocked at the door and cried: "Open the door, dear children. It is your mother – I have brought you something tasty to eat."

But the wolf put his black paws up to the window…

"No, we won't open the door!" the little kids shouted. "Our mother has white feet. You must be the wolf!"

Then the wolf loped off to a baker and stole a sack of flour. He scattered it over his feet till they were quite white, then he went for a third time to the house of the little kids.

Once more he knocked and cried: "Open the door, dear children. It is your mother – I have brought you something tasty to eat."

This time, his voice was soft and the paws he put up at the window were white.

Then the little kids believed what he said and opened the door.

The wolf leapt in!

The little kids scampered here and there, trying to hide. One sprang under the table, the second into bed, the third hid in the stove, the fourth ran into the kitchen, the fifth into the cupboard, the sixth under the washing-bowl, and the seventh into the grandfather clock. But the wolf found them. One by one, he swallowed them up – all except for the youngest in the clock.

Then the wolf felt full and uncomfortable. He staggered off and lay down under a tree, to sleep off his enormous meal.

Soon afterwards, the mother goat came home from the forest. What a sight she saw! The front door stood wide open. The table, chairs, and benches were tipped over, the washing-bowl lay broken to pieces, and the quilts and pillows were pulled off the bed. She searched and searched for her children, calling out their names, but they were

nowhere to be found. At last, the mother goat found the youngest kid trembling inside the grandfather clock. She took him out and he told her that the wolf had come and had eaten all the others.

How the mother goat wept over the loss of her poor kids!

Then she ran to find the wolf, and the youngest kid ran with her. They found the wolf lying under the tree, snoring loudly –

and something was moving inside his belly!

The mother goat's eyes opened wide. "Could my poor kids still be alive?" she gasped. She sent the little kid home to fetch scissors and a needle and thread. Then the mother goat gently cut open the wolf's stomach. *Pop! Pop! Pop! Pop! Pop! Pop!* Out sprang all six little kids! The wolf had been so greedy that he had swallowed them whole. The little kids brought big stones to the mother goat, who put them in the wolf's stomach and sewed him back up. She did it so carefully that he didn't feel a thing! Then back home they raced and bolted the door.

At length the wolf woke up. The stones in his stomach made him feel very thirsty and he wanted to go to the well to drink. As he walked, the stones knocked against each other and rattled inside him. He reached the well and stooped to take a drink – but the heavy stones tipped him over and he toppled in. The stones carried him down to the bottom and he drowned.

So that was the end of the wolf, and the seven little kids and their mother lived happily ever after.

Foundling

One day a huntsman was riding through a forest. Suddenly he heard the sound of a toddler screaming. He followed the cries to a tree and saw a little boy clinging to the topmost branch.

The man thought that an eagle must have picked the boy up from somewhere and carried him back to its nest. He climbed up the tree, took the crying child carefully in his arms, and said kindly, "Don't cry. I'll look after you. I will call you Foundling, because I found you. You will live with me and grow up with my little girl, Lina."

So that's what happened. As the years passed, the two children came to love each other dearly, and did everything together.

Now the huntsman had an old cook, called Sara, who was secretly a witch. One evening, Lina saw Sara carrying buckets back and forth from the spring, many times. "Why are you fetching so much water?" Lina asked.

"You must promise not to tell anyone!" said the old woman. "While your father is out in the forest tomorrow morning, I will brew a spell. I need lots of water to boil up my special ingredient – little boy." With that, the old woman shuffled off to fetch more water, cackling under her breath.

Next morning, the huntsman got up before sunrise and went out into the forest. Lina heard him leave – for she was so worried that she hadn't closed her eyes all night. She shook Foundling awake. "I will never leave you," she whispered to her brother.

"And I will never leave you," the little boy whispered back.

"Then trust me. Old Sara is a witch and

plans to kill you! We must run away – *now*."

So the two little children got dressed and slipped out of the house. By the time old Sara had got up and had set the huge pot of water to boil, they were well away into the forest.

When Sara crept into the children's bedroom and found them gone she was furious! She went straight to the huntsman's servant and told him that the children had run away, and he must fetch them back.

Before long, the little boy and girl heard footsteps chasing after them through the trees. In the blink of an eye, Foundling changed himself into a rose bush and Lina became a rose growing on it. And the servant raced right past them! How puzzled he was, when their footprints disappeared! There was nothing for him to do but traipse back home.

"Where are the children?" Sara screeched when the servant returned alone.

"Their footprints just led to a little rose bush with one rose on it," the servant said.

"You fool!" the old cook roared. "You should have cut the rose bush in two and brought it to me! I shall have to fetch them myself!" She set off, all the while muttering to herself about how stupid the servant was.

After a while, the children heard the old witch coming. In the blink of an eye, Foundling turned himself into a pond and Lina became a little duck floating on it.

When old Sara came huffing and puffing

up, she stopped for a moment at the pond to take a drink. As she leaned over the water, the duck seized the witch's hair in its beak and with one great heave, tugged her right into the water. The old witch drowned.

The children went home happily together to their father, and lived comfortably together for the rest of their days.